D0513019

Put Beginning Readers on the Right Track with ALL ABOARD READING™

The All Aboard Reading series is especially for beginning readers. Written by noted authors and illustrated in full color, these are books that children really and truly *want* to read—books to excite their imagination, tickle their funny bone, expand their interests, and support their feelings. With three different reading levels, All Aboard Reading lets you choose which books are most appropriate for your children and their growing abilities.

Level 1—for Preschool through First Grade Children
Level 1 books have very few lines per page, very large type, easy words, lots of repetition, and pictures with visual "cues" to help children figure out the words on the page.

Level 2—for First Grade to Third Grade Children
Level 2 books are printed in slightly smaller type than Level 1 books. The stories are more complex, but there is still lots of repetition in the text and many pictures. The sentences are quite simple and are broken up into short lines to make reading easier.

Level 3—for Second Grade through Third Grade Children
Level 3 books have considerably longer texts, use harder words and more complicated sentences.

All Aboard for happy reading!

For Rachael and Jonny Salami

Copyright © 1993 by Jon Buller and Susan Schade. All rights reserved. Published by Grosset & Dunlap, Inc., which is a member of The Putnam & Grosset Group, New York. ALL ABOARD READING is a trademark of The Putnam & Grosset Group. Published simultaneously in Canada. Printed in the U.S.A.

Library of Congress Cataloging-in-Publication Data

Buller, John, 1943-
Yo! It's captain yo-yo / by Jon Buller and Susan Schade.
p. cm. — (All aboard reading)
Summary: Steve finds a magic yo-yo in his attic and uses it to save Earth from being destroyed by the Blobs of Kazoo.
[1. Yo-yos—Fiction. 2. Magic—Fiction. 3. Science fiction.]
I. Schade, Susan. II. Title. III. Series.
PZ7.B9135Yo 1993
[E]—dc20 92-44306

ISBN 0-448-40191-6 A B C D E F G H I J

By Jon Buller and Susan Schade

Grosset & Dunlap • New York

I know what kids say about me.

They say, "Steve would forget his head if it wasn't stuck on his body."

But the truth is I remember more than they think I do.

Like the time I saved our planet! I'll never forget that.

It all started the day I went up in the attic to look for my mom's old comic books.

Our attic is full of neat stuff.

I saw Dad's old train set from when he was a kid. Mom's school yearbooks. My old crib. And my tricycle.

Now let's see—what did I come up here for in the first place?

I couldn't remember.

Oh, well. I figured it would come back to me in a few minutes.

I started poking around.

That's when I noticed the box. It was just a little square cardboard box tied up with string. But it seemed to be glowing inside.

I untied the string and opened the box.

Inside was . . . a YO-YO! But not your average yo-yo. This one was gold and it sparkled all over.

I picked it up. I slipped the string over my finger.

I let the yo-yo drop.

It purred like a cat and snapped back into my hand. Thwock! What a yo-yo!

I bounced it up and down a few times. And then I decided to try a trick I had seen my friend Curtis do.

It took me two hours to untangle the string.

When I was putting the yo-yo back in its box, I noticed a little piece of gold paper. I unfolded it and started to read.

As I read the last word—toy—the paper started to crumble. Little pieces fell through my fingers. Soon there was nothing left but a pile of gold-colored dust.

"Yeah, sure," I thought. "Hidden power! Secret word—I'll bet!"

Still, it wouldn't hurt to try.

I started to say the secret word, "Fizz..." I did not get any further. The yo-yo was burning my fingers!

"EEAGH!" I dropped it as fast as I could! That's when I began to think the yo-yo was for real. And I'd better save it for a <u>real</u> emergency.

Then I had an awful thought. What if I forgot the secret word? That would be just like me. So I made a drawing on the back of my library card to help me remember. It looked like this—🍾🍳. The 🍾 was for Fizz. And the 🍳 was for Pot.

I put my library card in my wallet.

I hoped there would be a real emergency soon!

1/4
3/4
1/3
2/3
SS

The next day I had to give an oral book report in school. I hate talking in front of the class.

It was my turn next.

My hands were sweaty and I was having trouble breathing.

I walked to the front of our classroom. "My book report is on...uh...uh..."

I couldn't even remember the name of the book!

"Uh, I forgot the title," I mumbled. "But it was a really good book."

Somebody laughed.

Lydia said loudly, "What else did you forget, Steve? Your brains?"

Lydia is the biggest know-it-all in our class. And a loudmouth, besides.

Now the whole class was laughing.

My ears were burning. My throat felt all tight. And I still had to give my book report.

It was a real emergency!

I reached for my golden yo-yo.

But before I could say the secret word, the PA system came on.

"ALL CLASSES REPORT TO THE AUDITORIUM RIGHT AWAY!"

I was off the hook!

The class marched down to the auditorium.

Mr. Reilly, our principal, was standing on the stage. "Students," he said, "I have a very sad announcement to make. Our school has been taken over by Blobs from space!"

"HA HA HA!" We all laughed.

The curtain opened behind Mr. Reilly. It wasn't a joke!

There really were Blobs from space! And a spaceship! The Blobs were all smooth and squishy-looking and their shapes kept changing in a very creepy way.

Everyone was speechless.

Except Mr. Reilly. "The following after-school activities will be canceled, due to the invasion," he said. "Chess Club, Baseball Card Swap, Video Game Club, basketball tryouts, field hockey practice..."

One of the Blobs shoved Mr. Reilly out of the way. "All right, already," he said in a slimy, gurgly voice. "I've got something to say." Chomp, chomp. He seemed to be chewing gum.

"We come from the planet Kazoo. And I've got to tell you guys, this is one crummy planet. Everybody else in the universe is more advanced than you. And you don't even know it!"

He chomped on his gum and glared at us.

"And you know what else?" he suddenly shouted. "Your stupid little planet is getting in our way! Every night at exactly ten o'clock your orbit blocks our TV reception. And that makes us mad." Chomp, chomp.

"So we're going to wipe out Earth. We're going to squash everyone like bugs. And we're starting at your school first. Heh heh heh."

When the Blob laughed he jiggled like Jell-O. It was really gross.

I felt in my pocket for my yo-yo. The time had come to see what it could do!

Then Lydia stood up.

"I don't believe it," she said. "What can you do to us? You don't even have opposable thumbs!"

Mr. Reilly was shaking his head and making sit-down motions with his hands. But Lydia was just getting going.

"I'll bet your planet isn't advanced at all," she said. "I'll bet you copied your spaceship from one of our old science-fiction movies."

The Blob blew a big bubble with his gum.

It floated down and landed on Lydia.

"Hey!" she cried.

The bubble oozed over her like a giant runny egg until she was completely covered.

"Umf, umf," we heard. And we could see her kicking and punching for a few seconds.

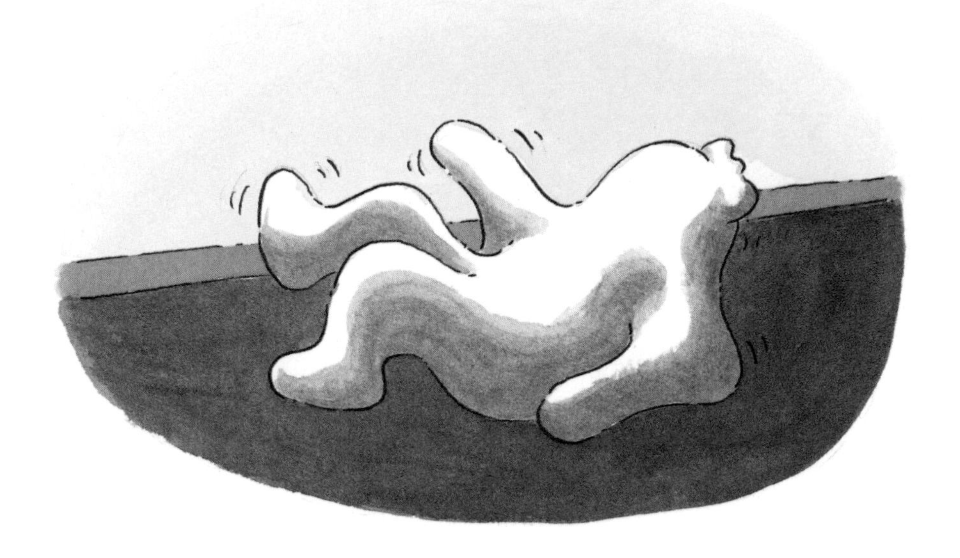

Then she was gone. And in her place was a smooth new girl Blob. She slimed up on the stage with the other Blobs.

I gulped and raised my hand.

"What do you want?" the head Blob asked me. "The bubble treatment?"

I shook my head. "Can I go to the boys' room?" I croaked.

"No!" the Blob said.

"But I really <u>have</u> to!"

"All right, all right. Make it quick."

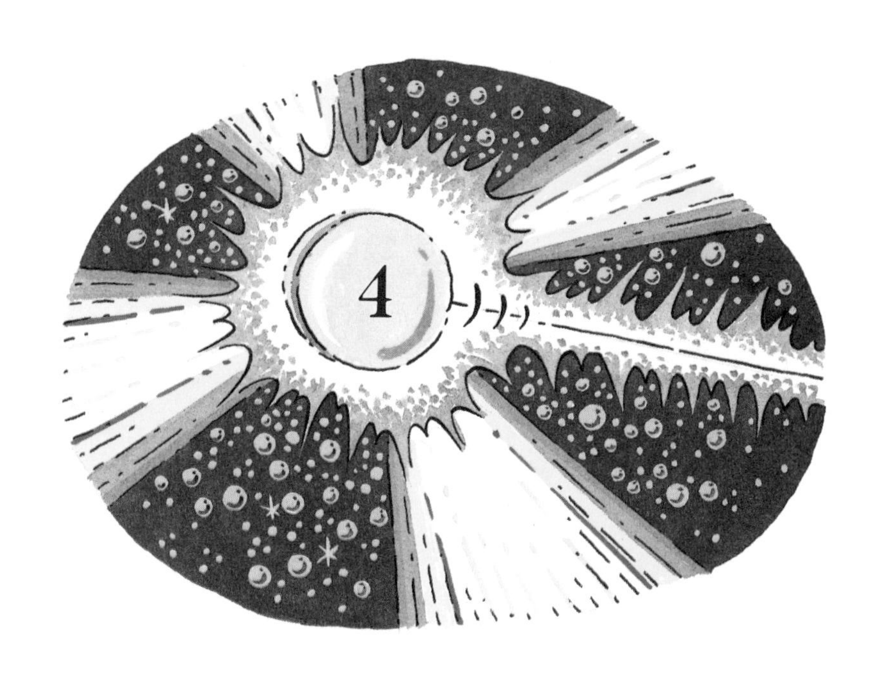

In the boys' room I took out my golden yo-yo and my library card. I looked at the drawing I had made to help me remember the secret word.

"HATDRIP!" I said.

Nothing happened.

I looked at the drawing again. I turned the card around.

"SODABUCKET!" I tried.

Nothing happened.

Then I remembered! "FIZZPOT!" I cried.

There was a blinding flash!

And I was Captain Yo-Yo! At least there was a big, good-looking guy in a superhero suit looking back at me in the mirror.

I spun my yo-yo a few times. It was humming and glowing.

I did a few yo-yo tricks. Wow! There was nothing I couldn't do. Around-the-world, rocking-the-cradle, twisting-the-pretzel!

I walked the dog all the way back to the auditorium.

"YO!" I shouted. "It's me, Captain Yo-Yo, to the rescue!"

"Yeah, right," said the Lydia Blob. "You look like a sick joke. Go back to the Saturday morning cartoons where you belong."

Being a Blob hadn't changed Lydia much.

"Yo! Watch this!" I said. I flashed my yo-yo in front of her a few times.

"Wow!" shouted some kids. "The guy is really good!"

I put on quite a show. My yo-yo glowed and hummed. Over and under, back and forth. It sparkled and sizzled.

All the kids watched. So did the Blobs. In fact, they couldn't take their eyes off the yo-yo. Back and forth, over and under. Soon their eyelids started to droop.

Then it hit me. I was putting the whole room under a spell! That was the yo-yo's hidden power.

"You are getting sleepy," I said. I did my trick in slow motion. "Very sleepy."

It was working!

"You are totally in my control," I said, neatly catching the yo-yo in my hand. All of the Blobs looked at me with half-closed eyes.

"Yes, Master," they said.

"Yes, Master," Mr. Reilly said.

"Yes, Master," all the kids said.

Wow! What power! I had almost forgotten about everyone else. I couldn't resist a little test. "Repeat after me," I said. "Yo, Steve! You are the greatest!"

"Yo, Steve! You are the greatest!" the whole room roared.

"Louder!"

"YO, STEVE! YOU ARE THE GREATEST!"

It was nice of them to say so.

"All right," I said. "It's time for the Blobs to go back to Kazoo."

"Yes, Exalted Boss." They all bowed. Even Lydia.

"When you get there you will remember nothing except this: Earth is the most advanced planet you ever saw. And you were lucky to escape with your lives. No Blob will watch television after ten at night. And you will never come back. You may go now."

And away they went! They lined up and oozed toward their spaceship.

But then I remembered Lydia.

Should I save her, or shouldn't I?

I should.

"WAIT!" I yelled. "Lydia must stay here!"

The Lydia Blob came back. She stood in front of me. The ooze melted away. And there was the old Lydia looking sticky and grouchy.

I watched the Blobs slide into their spaceship and take off. I waved to them. "Yo! Have a nice day," I yelled.

Then I said to the kids and the teachers, "In five minutes you will wake up. You will remember none of this."

And I zipped back to the boys' room.

I took one last look in the mirror, and said the secret word, "SODASTEW!"

Hmm. I guess that wasn't it...What <u>was</u> that word?

Oh, yeah. "FIZZPOT!"

In a flash, I was me again.

When I got back, everyone was saying, "Where are we? What's happening?"

Nobody remembered anything!

Except, of course, me!